A Most Unusual Dog

Tohby Riddle

Gareth Stevens Publishing
MILWAUKEE

For a free color catalog describing Gareth Stevens' list of high-quality books, call 1-800-341-3569 (USA) or 1-800-461-9120 (Canada).

For my parents

ISBN 0-8368-1088-0

North American edition first published in 1994 by
Gareth Stevens Publishing
1555 North RiverCenter Drive, Suite 201
Milwaukee, Wisconsin 53212, USA

This edition © 1994 by Tohby Riddle. First published in Australia
in 1992 by The Macmillan Company of Australia Pty. Ltd. Original
© 1992 by Tohby Riddle.

Printed in the United States of America

1 2 3 4 5 6 7 8 9 99 98 97 96 95 94

Fletcher was a rather unusual dog.
It wasn't just that he preferred pancakes
to dog biscuits . . .

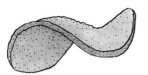

it was that he cooked them himself.

Nor was it that he lived in a dog house.
That was quite common . . .

except that he built it with his
own two paws.

Not only was Fletcher allowed on the couch, he had chosen the upholstery.

While other dogs barked at the moon,
Fletcher studied it through his telescope,
such was his interest in astronomy.

For many dogs,
a visit to the park
would mean
chasing cyclists . . .

but not for Fletcher.

If the neighbors had a complaint to make about Fletcher, it wasn't that he kept them awake all night by barking . . .

but that he played his Bing Crosby
records too loud.

Such a dog inevitably
attracted a lot of attention.

Overnight, Fletcher became a star . . .

even a movie star.

His picture was everywhere.

Soon, everyone wanted to know Fletcher or at least be seen with him.

He became the favorite of every
society hostess.

So while most dogs spent
their evenings rummaging
through garbage cans or
chewing on a shoe . . .

Fletcher was visiting clubs . . .

presenting awards . . .

or attending the opera.

But Fletcher was,
after all, a dog.

One evening, while Fletcher
was the special guest at a dinner
on a harbor cruise . . .

he was spotted by someone from
the dog pound.

There was a brief scuffle . . .

but Fletcher swam to freedom.

As for the rest of
the story, no one
really knows.

Some say he went on to become the first dog in space . . .

while others say Fletcher ended up in
a cottage somewhere on the coast with
an old fisherman . . . and a most
unusual cat.